Butter

A Chinese Legend of Star-Crossed Lovers

A Novella

Teresa Ng

Butterfly Dreams is a work of historical fiction. Apart from the recorded historical people, events, and locales that mixed into the narrative; all names, characters, places, and incidents are the products of the author's imagination or are used fictitiously.

This book is dedicated to
my husband Joseph,
who once gifted me these precious words.

* * *

A Moment of Pause at Highland

Cherish our relationship,
treasure the days we have;
much to be grateful for.

April 1, 2010

* * *

Table of Contents

In the Peach Orchard of the Jade Empress
One Late Summer Day During Ming Dynasty on Earth (1368-
1644)

The day started out balmy in the morning, but quickly became hot and muggy by early afternoon, and a thin drizzle was falling. The pair of Monarch butterflies with the duty of patrolling the peach orchard for the Jade Empress became tired. They had been flying around the peach trees since early morning, making sure no birds or insects attempted to eat or mar the velvety skin of the golden fruits ripening under the sun. In case of trouble, the guardian dragons in their nearby caves could be summoned quickly by sound waves emitting from the tips of their wings.

"Ai-ya!" Butterfly Girl said to her companion, "My wings feel so sticky and heavy. I think they might fall off shortly if I don't stop and take a rest!"

"You women are always complaining!" Butterfly Boy snorted and for emphasis, he flapped his wings rapidly several times. "You go ahead and take a nap on a leaf in the shade. I'll continue patrolling by myself!"

Butterfly Girl flew away in a huff. She was feeling too tired to argue with that arrogant male! After circling a few fragrant smelling fruits, she landed on a leafy surface under one of them. Folding together her fragile tawny and black colored wings, she fell asleep within seconds.

After a long interval, Butterfly Boy became tired also and felt lonely without the pretty girlfriend flying by his side. He went and looked for her and found her snoring gently on a leaf right under the juiciest golden peach. Heaving a deep sigh, he covered her with his right wing and went napping next to her.

All was peaceful and quiet in the peach orchard.

The monkeys from Wah Mountain came. They were unusually quiet for monkeys. Their leader, a young male with reddish fur and a pinched cunning face, kept them quiet by swishing his skinny long tail on top of their heads. They were a hungry bunch craving for a taste of juicy treats. Avoiding the few peach trees in proximity to the caves of the guardian dragons, they circled and nimbly climbed up the rest of them.

Within no more than a heartbeat, most of the juicy and fragrant peaches were chomped up by the monkeys, who had been waiting for this opportunity for a long time in a nearby forest. At last feeling replete with full stomachs of delicious fruits, they forgot caution and started their noisy chattering.

The pair of Monarch butterflies were awakened rudely by sticky juices dripping down on their bodies. Butterfly Boy flapped his right wing off his girlfriend's back and helped her to unglue and to extend her wings. They struggled to their legs and flew up together from the wet and sticky leafy surface. Once in the air, they let loose sound waves from the tips of their wings to summon the guardian dragons.

Swinging from tree to tree, the monkeys quickly fled from the guardian dragons. A few unlucky ones were caught and ended up as lunch for the ferocious breasts. They left the orchard a mess. The peaches left on the few untouched trees would not be enough to make fruit brandy for the consumption of the Jade Empress, her husband and their immortals.

"What punishment would be fitting for these two Monarch butterflies, who slept while on watch duty in my peach orchard?" The Jade Empress asked her husband, who became grumpy trying to lick the last drop of peach brandy from his golden chalice.

"Send them down to Earth!" Roared the Jade Emperor, who was very fond of his daily quota of delicious liquor. "Let them suffer as humans there!"

"But, who will patrol the peach orchard meanwhile?"

"You don't need patrols right now, there are no peaches left! Besides, they'll only be gone for a moment. Remember, one day up here is a thousand years down there on Earth!"

Thus, poor Butterfly Boy and Butterfly Girl had their wings ripped off their backs before they were banished from Heaven.

6

Chapter – 1

The Scholarly Maiden

Madam Zhu had her first argument with her husband and she felt horrified by her own daring. She and Squire Zhu had been married these past thirty-three years since she was a shy maiden of sixteen. She had always respected his shrewdness and good judgment, especially proud of their famous Shaoxing wineries of excellent rice wine production. However, she just could not accept his prejudiced view concerning their one and only child – talented sixteen years old daughter Yingtai.

She shuddered at the memory of their earlier confrontation.

"What do you mean we should allow Yingtai to travel to Hangzhou to further her education?" Huffed Squire Zhu, his face became alarmingly red. "Have you forgotten that we have a daughter, not a son?"

"Old Lord, of course I know Yingtai is a girl!" Madam Zhu felt intimidated by her husband's anger, but her desire to champion their daughter's cause spurred her on. "But times have changed and we should not hold her back from achieving her potential just because of her gender!"

"I absolutely forbid her to leave home for any reason! A beautiful young maiden such as our daughter would bring dishonor to our family name if her virtue is ever being questioned!"

"Ha! You think Yingtai is beautiful?"

"Yes! But her beauty is not typical of our time. Her facial features are distinctly chiseled and she is too tall for a girl. In the company of her peers, our Yingtai resembles a pure white chrysanthemum standing amidst multicolored blooms!"

"Well, since no one other than her own father thinks she is beautiful; will it be alright for Yingtai to go to Hangzhou with a chaperone?"

"No! Just forget about this nonsense!" Squire Zhu stared at his wife so hard, making her wondered if she had suddenly sprouted

7

horns on her head. "Unless the girl could successfully disguise herself as a man, so that even her own parents can't recognize her!"

Madam Zhu became thoughtful at his remark.

The subject of their heated argument was at the moment sitting in the back garden, blissfully painting a picture of butterflies dancing among flowers. Her father was right; Zhu Yingtai definitely could not qualify as a beauty in their current society. The latest trend favored a short, sloping-shoulder silhouette, slanted eyes and a small rosebud mouth on a soft round face. She was tall and slim, with large bright eyes like two pools of clear spring water on an oval face, and a shapely mobile mouth made for laughter. However, her looks mattered not a whit to Yingtai, whose passion for learning surpassed anything most young maidens thought important and proper.

"Oh! How I wish Papa would allow me to study under Master Chow Ming in Hangzhou!" Yingtai said to Rensum, her personal maidservant who stood behind her. "He is considered to be the best teacher advocating liberal thoughts and reforms for our society, and I have read several articles written by him on those subjects!"

Her pretty maidservant responded with a chuckle, "Young Miss, I think you should just forget about your fantasy of attending school away from home. It is unheard of for a girl! Anyway, since your sixteenth birthday, there have been numerous matchmakers approaching your parents, asking for your hand in marriage to sons of their clients. So far, Old Lord and Old Mistress have declined for one reason or the other. However, one of these days they will break down and choose a husband for you. I think you might as well start sewing a trousseau instead of wasting time wishing for the impossible!"

"What? You want me to just embroider and sew all day long, rather than to improve my mind by reading, writing, painting, and practicing calligraphy?"

"Young Miss, I might not be as smart as you are, but I do know embroidering and sewing are more suitable tasks for women! What are you going to use all your book learning for after marriage when you have to manage your household and rear your children?"

"Well! By being able to read and write, no one will be able to cheat me on household purchases, and I will be able to save plenty of money by not needing to hire a tutor for my children!"

"No wonder Old Lord likes to say: Ignorance is a virtue in women!" Rensum shrugged her shoulders, finally gave up trying to convince her beloved Young Miss to know her place as a woman.

Just then Madam Zhu came into the garden, followed by her personal maidservant Dongmui, carrying a large tray of food and drink.

"Yingtai, come eat lunch with me inside the gazebo!" Madam Zhu looked over her daughter's painting with appreciation; the butterflies and flowers painted on the silken panel appearing so real, that they blended in naturally with the scenery of the garden.

"Yes, Mama!" Yingtai laid down her brush and carefully covered up the tiny paint pots on the small table. "Where is Papa? Isn't he coming to eat with us?"

"Your father is having lunch in town today with some friends, no doubt talking business as usual!" Madam Zhu answered her daughter. Then she turned to the two maidservants and said: "You two youngsters go to eat in the kitchen. Cook has made plenty of streamed barbecue pork buns and fried shrimp crescents today!"

"Thank you, Old Mistress!" Happily, the two young girls held hands and ran off just as they were bidden by their kind mistress, who treated her household workers like members of her family.

Mother and daughter enjoyed a leisurely meal by themselves inside the gazebo.

That evening, as Squire Zhu and his wife sat in their front courtyard enjoying the fresh breeze before retiring to bed, they heard the tinkling sounds of the soothsayer's bell outside their door.

"Dongmui, go invite the holy man in. We haven't had our fortune told for ages!" Madam Zhu bade her personal maidservant, who sat idly on a stool at her feet playing cat's cradle with a red hair cord. In response, Dongmui slipped the piece of red string inside her pocket and went skipping out the door.

"My Lady," Squire Zhu glared at his wife to show his disapproval. "Why do you women always fall for the lies of these charlatans? Don't you know they just want to empty your purse of coins?"

"Old Lord, don't be so stingy! Just to be on the safe side; I would rather believe, than not believe the words of a holy man!" Madam Zhu smiled sweetly to her husband and laughed out loud when he rolled his eyes at her.

Dongmui came back followed by a young man wearing a black robe, with the silver emblem of eternity embroidered on the chest. He carried a white banner with words of 'Living Immortal' written in bold black letters on it, and a young boy walked behind him shaking a small bell.

The soothsayer bowed low to Squire Zhu and Madam Zhu: "My Lord and My Lady. I am at your service! What do you wish me to forecast for you today?"

"Tell me about the coming harvest." Squire Zhu asked gruffly. "Will it be bountiful this autumn?"

The soothsayer looked up to the sky, closed his eyes and mumbled a string of incoherent words to himself. In cue, the boy danced around him ringing the small bell.

"My Lord," the soothsayer stopped his mumbling, opened his eyes and bowed to Squire Zhu. "I predict with the exception of several fields located at the edge of the forest, you will have a bumper rice crop from your hundreds of acres before the end of this year!"

Squire Zhu looked at the soothsayer with suspicion. No one other than people within his family knew that he had used several fields next to the forest for experimenting a new method of rice planting; hoping to double the yield from the land. He had just ordered his farmhands to turn the soil in those fields and to sow already sprouted rice seedlings from one of his warehouses. In the future, an extra rice harvest would allow him to produce more rice wine in his wineries for the market. How had this young man found out? Was he a spy from his business competitors trying to steal his production secrets?

"You rascal!" Turning red in the face, Squire Zhu rose from the chair, picked up his cane and hit the soothsayer with it while his wife looked on in horror. "Who has paid you to worm into my affairs? No one other than my family members and trusted farm workers know anything about what I am doing with the fields located at the edge of the forest!"

The soothsayer nimbly ducked under Squire Zhu's cane, but it knocked off the cone shaped, black lawn hat from his head. He straightened up quickly to face his attacker; shook loose a cascade of silky, hip-length black hair and pulled the pair of whiskers from his face. What Squire Zhu saw leaving him totally in shock.

"Papa! Don't hit me! Look, I am your daughter Yingtai!"

"You naughty girl! How dare you trying to fool me, your own father?"

"I have to, Papa! I need to convince you to allow me to attend school in Hangzhou! Mama told me earlier you would agree, if I could disguise myself ably as a man, so that even you could not recognize me!"

Squire Zhu turned and scowled at his wife, who looked sheepish but stubbornly tilted her chin up to her husband. He knew he was losing the battle against the fair sex of his household.

"Old Lord, those were your very own words!" For the shake of their beloved daughter's happiness, Madam Zhu was not going to give in to her husband's prejudice against women any longer. "I think Yingtai deserves the chance to obtain higher education!"

The thus far being ignored young boy came up and knelt down before Squire Zhu, kowtowed to him and pulled off the cotton cap from his head. Squire Zhu suffered another shock seeing his daughter's personal maidservant Rensum appeared in front of him.

"Old Lord," Pleaded Rensum to Squire Zhu. "Please allow me to accompany Young Miss to Hangzhou! I promise you I'll take good care of her!"

"Enough!" Roared Squire Zhu. "Leave me alone, all of you! I need time to think this over!"

Everyone, including Madam Zhu, wisely left the poor besieged man sitting alone in the front courtyard.

"Oh! I still can't believe Papa actually allows me to attend school in Hangzhou!" said Yingtai to her mother, who was busily helping her to pack for her journey. Madam Zhu had spent a whole week shopping for her daughter: picking out several pairs of sturdy men's shoes with thickly glued cloth soles, a pair of oil-cloth boots for foul weather, scholar's triangular cotton scarves in several fashionable colors, and a couple of folded paper fans with painted sceneries suitable for the use of young men. Fearing gossip, she dared not ask the seamstress in town to make male outfits for their daughter and her maidservant. So, to his husband's chagrin, she cut down almost half of his wardrobe to fit Yingtai's slender figure and took from his warehouse several sets of plain cotton clothing normally reserved for young farm workers to outfit Rensum. She folded and placed everything neatly inside two reed baskets she had purchased and closed the lids with relief.

"Well, I am glad everything fits in these two light weight baskets! I don't think Rensum will be able to carry heavier ones on her shoulder pole all the way to Hangzhou!"

"Mama, I will help her with them. After all, she is going there for my sake!"

"Daughter, I am glad you have the right attitude. I feel very proud of you!"

"Thank you, Mama, for everything you have done for me!"

"No need to thank me. Just study hard and be a good girl!"

Forgetting decorum, Yingtai gave her mother a tight hug. Madam Zhu felt her heart bursting with tenderness for her beloved only child, who would shortly be living her own long ago, secret dream of being a female scholar.

Chapter – 2

On the Road to Hangzhou

It was a mid-autumn morning when Yingtai, in the guise of a young scholar and her maidservant Rensum as her book-valet, set out from their home in the suburb of Shaoxing town on the road to Hangzhou, thirty-seven miles away. The day was balmy but a bit warmer than usual, which tired Rensum out quickly. She had the pair of loaded reed baskets she was balancing on the pole across her thin shoulders.

"Rensum," Yingtai said with concern to her maidservant, seeing beads of sweat on her brow. "Let me take the load off you for a while. You have been carrying these baskets for the past three hours!"

"Oh, no, Young Miss!" Rensum protested vehemently. "What will anyone think of me: a lazy, no good book-valet neglecting his duty? Besides, you'll look ridiculous shouldering these two reed baskets in your scholar's long robe!"

"You don't have to be concerned. We have not encountered anyone on this lonely road since we left home!" Yingtai tried to ply the pole off her maidservant's shoulders. "And don't address me anymore as Young Miss, I am Young Master to you from now on!"

"Alright, Young Master!" Rensum giggled and with a sigh of relief she slipped the pole with the hanging reed baskets off her shoulders. Then she straightened up and pointed to a small structure beyond a stand of trees. "Look! We can take our rest in that farewell gazebo and eat the lunch Old Mistress packed for us. I am starving, aren't you?"

"Hungry Ghost!" Yingtai laughed at her maidservant, who always had a healthy appetite. "Let's go there to rest for a short while and see what delicious dim-sums Mama has wrapped up for us!"

Quickly, Rensum shouldered the pole with the pair of reed baskets again and skipped towards the farewell gazebo like a rabbit. Laughing gaily, Yingtai picked up the hem of her long robe to keep up with her.

Reaching the farewell gazebo, both Yingtai and Rensum were dismayed to find it had already been occupied. A young scholar and his manservant were sitting at the round stone table inside the tiny structure, eating their noon meal.

"Rensum, I think we should continue our way to find another spot to eat lunch!" Yingtai whispered to her disappointed companion, who was clearly exhausted and hungry as well.

Just then the young scholar turned and called out to them, "Please don't leave, but join us for a bite to eat! The next rest spot is at least two more hours away!"

Reluctantly, Yingtai and Rensum left their reed baskets outside, entered the gazebo and seated themselves on the extra stone stools at the stone table. The young scholar smiled his welcome, but his rough looking manservant gave them a dark scowl.

"Young Master," said the manservant gruffly. "We have hardly enough food for ourselves to be sharing with strangers!"

"Please pardon my man Sigull," the young scholar apologized to Yingtai. "He always acts grouchy when he is feeling tired and hungry! Here, take a pair of chopsticks and try some of these meat dumplings!"

"Thank you!" Yingtai picked up a dumpling with the chopsticks and took a small bite. "Um…delicious! Rensum, why don't you go get the dim-sums from the reed basket and we'll share them with our new friends here?"

Rensum returned with a large lotus leave wrapped bundle, laid it down on the stone table and opened it up. It was a mouthwatering feast that laid out in front of them. Yingtai's mother had packed some of the most favorite dim-sums for her daughter's journey: steamed shrimp dumplings, baked barbecue pork buns, sweet water chestnut jellied squares, and fried sticky rice balls stuffed with sugared lotus seed paste and covered with sesame seeds.

Feeling relaxed and at ease after eating the delicious lunch, they began introducing each other before parting their ways.

"My given name is Shanbo from the house of Liang." Said the young scholar to Yingtai. "I am on my way to Hangzhou to study under Master Chow Ming."

"Oh! How wonderful! I have also been accepted by Master Chow Ming and am on my way to join him!" Said Yingtai, who could not help but noticing how handsome and tall her lunch companion was, with large intelligent eyes and a bright smile. "I am Yingtai from

14

the house of Zhu. Why don't we keep each other company on the road to Hangzhou?"

"I am indeed overjoyed to have you as my traveling companion! We can relief the tedium by deliberating various new innovative thoughts of Chow Lo-shi (Teacher)!" Liang Shanbo was also delighted by his newfound friend's pleasing appearance: finely chiseled facial features and delicate body built, like a jade tree standing in the wind.

Yingtai and Shanbo walked together ahead, enjoying each other's company while Rensum and Sigull followed behind them, jostling each other with their baskets.

"Are you always such a bully?" Gasped Rensum to Sigull, she looked like she was ready to cry. "Look what you have done to my arm! It will be black and blue for days!"

"Aw, I am so sorry!" Sigull finally relented, put down his baskets and took ahold of Rensum's arm. He pulled up her sleeve to inspect the damage his jostling had done and was alarmed to see he had caused a large welt on the pale tender flesh. He rubbed and blew on the reddening lump vigorously while Rensum struggled to free her arm from his overzealous ministering.

"Don't bother anymore! I am sure it will be alright shortly!" Rensum blushed furiously, she had never been touched by a man, especially one so virile looking. "I am surprised Young Master Liang has you as his book-valet, you don't look the type at all!"

"Book-valet? I am the only servant left in the Liang household ever since Old Lord passed away last winter! Poor Old Mistress can't even afford to pay me because her late husband was a minor official who had two sleeves full of clean breeze. He was too honest for his own good, you understand? I elected to stay with her out of gratitude since she had rescued me as an abandoned infant and raised me like her own kin."

"Well, I am honored to keep company with such a good fellow like you!" Rensum said shyly, her young girl's heart was touched. "Let us be friends, alright?"

"Yes, indeed! I'll treat you like a younger brother if you don't mind?" Sigull abruptly gave Rensum a bear hug, noticing this lad's body was too soft. She struggled to free herself from his strangling hold, turned red in the face and finally bit his arm to make him let her go.

15

"Ouch!" Sigull rubbed his wounded arm and frowned at his new friend. "Is this the way you show appreciation for my brotherly love?"

"Well, you are simply too rough! I won't bite if you keep your distance from now on!"

Sigull shrugged his shoulders, picked up his load and walked ahead of Rensum. Feeling chastened, she followed him and called his name softly every once so often until he turned his head and gave her a sheepish smile.

Thus, they kept peace and reached the bustling city before dusk.

Chapter – 3

Master Chow's Boarding House

Led by Liang Shanbo, who had previously visited Hangzhou, the group of tired travelers arrived at Master Chow Ming's boarding house, located right next to the school, just in time for the evening meal.

"Please leave your baskets here in the courtyard, I'll have them put inside your rooms for you. You all must be exhausted. Come in and join us to eat the late-rice!" They were greeted warmly by Madam Chow; their teacher's elderly wife was a plump and kindly looking woman.

There were two large round tables set up inside the dining room. Madam Chow led them first to one of them where her husband Chow Ming sat among his family members, drinking a cup of tea.

"Old Lord, here are two more of your students and their servants who have just arrived!" Madam Chow proudly introduced the young scholars and indicated with her hand that they should kneel down to pay homage to their teacher. Liang Shanbo and Zhu Yingtai quickly obeyed her and went down on their knees, both knocked their heads thrice before Master Chow. Rensum and Sigull also did the same behind them.

"Very good! Very good!" Master Chow's winkled face crumpled in a broad smile and his gnarled thin fingers reached up to smooth the few long silvery beards on his pointed chin. "Get up! Get up! Go and join your fellow schoolmates to eat the late-rice. Your servants can eat inside the kitchen with our cook and servers."

Obediently, Shanbo and Yingtai went to the second table to sit down with eight other fellow students. They introduced each other briefly before the servers brought in steamy bowls of food. The only student struck in Yingtai's mind was the one who had also come from her hometown: Minchoy of the House of Ma, whose father owned the only silver exchange and pawnshop in Shaoxing. Yingtai thought Minchoy friendly and quite good looking, perhaps a bit spoiled in his flippant mannerism.

17

Even though Yingtai was exhausted from the daylong trip, she was hungry enough to enjoy the hearty meal laid out in front of her. They served a large tureen of winter melon soup with bits of ham and lotus seeds; slices of chicken meat stir-fried with peanuts and bamboo shoots in sweet chili sauce; chunks of roasted pork with the crispy skin on them; two large whole carps steamed with slices of ginger, scallion and black mushroom; vegetable dishes of bok-choy, lotus roots and bitter melons sautéed lightly with peanut oil and salt. A huge bowl of fluffily cooked brown rice and a tray of honey cake completed the wonderful meal for the hungry young scholars.

When the evening meal was over, Madam Chow told Yingtai and Shanbo to follow her to a bedroom upstairs that they would be sharing. Shanbo was thrilled to have Yingtai as a roommate, but she was stunned by Madam Chow's announcement and quickly pulled the elderly lady aside to question her.

"Madam Chow, please forgive me for contradicting you!" Yingtai pleaded. "But my father had received a letter from Master Chow only a week ago, confirming there would be a private bedroom reserved just for me and my book-valet. This has to be a mistake!"

The elderly lady was visibly embarrassed by her husband's broken promise to this young scholar, who seemed so upset having to share a bedroom.

"Young Master Zhu, I am so very sorry! I know my husband did promise your father a private bedroom for your use. Unfortunately, several more last-minute admissions turned up which he was unable to refuse without hurt feeling. We now have a total of ten students but only five bedrooms in this boarding house to share; three upstairs and two down here. There is no more space for sleeping anywhere else. Even your servant and Young Master Liang's servant will have to sleep on pallets on the floor beside your double bed. Come! Be a good boy and go upstairs with your friend. He is waiting anxiously for you!"

The elderly lady turned to lead her charges upstairs to their bedroom. With no choice, Yingtai picked up the hem of her long robe to follow, all the while praying to Guanyin, the Goddess of Mercy, to rescue her from this dire predicament.

"Younger Brother Zhu, why are you still up? It's getting awfully late!" Shanbo yawned, the daylong journey had tired him out. He had already curled up under his light quilt on one side of the double bed while his servant Sigull snored loudly from the pallet on the floor next to him.

"Sorry, Elder Brother Liang! I really enjoy reading this book, 'Three Hundred Poems from the Tang Dynasty', that I am not feeling sleepy yet!" The truth was; the poor maiden felt extremely tired but did not know what to do. She could not possibly share a bed with a man without having her womanly virtue compromised! In desperation, she drooped against the desk fighting fatigue with a book while her maidservant Rensum slept soundly on the pallet at her feet.

Shanbo was really getting annoyed with his new friend, now also roommate and schoolmate. He hopped out of bed and scooped Yingtai up into his arms. "I don't care what you enjoy doing! I only know you won't be able to wake up to attend class come morning, if you don't get some sleep now!"

"Put me down!" Yingtai struggled in Shanbo's arms so vigorously that he had to let go of her. "I'll come to bed by myself. However, you must stay on your side of the bed as far away from me as possible. I am not used to sleeping next to another person!"

"Well, I am not either! But we have no choice right now but to share this room for all four of us. Don't be so childish, Yingtai! You aren't living at home anymore!"

Yingtai felt trapped. She knew there could be no way to keep the secret of her gender from Shanbo if they shared the bed, even though this was a very wide double bed. What could she do?

She frantically looked around and finally spotted the pitcher of water with a stack of bowls sitting on a small corner table. Aha! She had found the solution to keep her secret from the handsome bedmate!

Shanbo felt incredulous when he saw Yingtai placed a bowl of water on the middle of their bed. "What are you doing? You want to get the bed all wet? I am too tired and sleepy to play games with you!"

"I am not playing games with you either! I just want you to stay as far away from me as possible. If you keep to your side, I guaranteed you will not get wet!"

Shanbo was simply too tired to deal with his new friend's antics anymore. So, he turned his back to Yingtai, wrapped himself tighter with the light quilt and fell instantly asleep.

With a sigh of relief, Yingtai gingerly climbed up into the bed and laid down next to the bowl of water.

She heard Rensum mumbled her disapproval from below. "Young Miss, what have you gotten yourself into now? Why don't we just go home tomorrow?"

Yingtai whispered back, "It's too late to quit! Papa has already paid a year's tuition to Master Chow. If I give up now, I'll never have another chance to attend school again!"

It was a miracle that the bowl of water on the bed remained full at cockcrow.

Chapter – 4

In Praise of Women

Dawn came all too soon. Shanbo was amazed to discover that his younger bedmate had already finished his morning ablution in the one and only bath chamber downstairs and also properly dressed for the day. He still felt tired to the bone and eyed the bowl of water sitting on the middle of the bed with irritation.

"Younger Brother Zhu, please take that blasted bowl of water out of the bed! If the chambermaid sees it, I am sure she will report to Madam Chow that we are lunatics!"

"Alright! Alright! Elder Brother Liang, I'll throw out this bowl of water right now! But please remember, another bowl of water will be placed on the same spot tonight!"

Shanbo scowled at Yingtai, thought he had to be a spoiled son from a rich family. Then he remembered how deliciously soft his new friend's body felt within his arms when he attempted to forcefully put him in bed last evening and he scowled even darker. "Oh, no!" He chastised himself. "This is ridicules! I have never felt the desire for another man's body before!"

He went ahead to strip off his pajamas and was astonished to see Yingtai turned red in the face and left their bedroom in a hurry. He shook his head and muttered, "That boy is simply too young to be living away from home. He needs his mother or a nanny to take care of him!"

Poor Yingtai stood outside the bedroom door quivering with a mixture of embarrassment and pleasure. She had seen the naked body of a man for the first time in her life! Oh! How beautiful he was without a stitch on, all firm muscles and straight limbs! She felt heat spreading over both her face and belly and walked downstairs to the kitchen on shaky legs. She looked so dazed that Cook asked her if she wanted to eat breakfast right away. She told the kindly woman that she would wait for her roommate.

Shanbo came down for breakfast. He noticed as soon as Yingtai met his eyes, his face crimsoned like a red camellia. He shrugged his

21

shoulders and wondered again what had he done that was affecting his new friend so strangely.

After a light breakfast of rice porridge, topped with pickled vegetables and small chunks of roasted pork; they left for their first day of school.

With anticipation Yingtai went with Shanbo to Master Chow's classroom next-door. The bookshelves lined room was not big, just a conversion of the family guest hall. However, two rows of desks and stools were neatly placed there like sentinels. It was still early and no one else was there yet, so they were able to pick two desks in front, sitting next to each other. Yingtai was glad that she would be close to Shanbo even in the classroom, she already felt an irresistible attachment to her handsome classmate; both mind and body.

Soon the room was filled up with noisy, enthusiastic students. They were mostly young men from families nearby, except Liang Shanbo, Zhu Yingtai and Ma Minchoy, who all came from Shaoxing. After a round of friendly shoulder slapping, they settled down to await the arrival of their teacher.

Master Chow arrived with two servants. The servants carried a large box of supplies and a jar of water. Each student was given a notepad, a brush, an inkwell and a stick of black ink. One of the servants filled each inkwell with water and the other servant made ink by stirring the water with the inksticks. Class was ready to begin.

The first assignment given by Master Chow was for them to write a short essay; indicating their aims for higher education. Most young men wrote their goals were to pass the official examinations, in order to obtain lucrative imperial appointments and to bestow honor and riches for their families. Shanbo said he wanted to improve his mind and be able to provide for his mother. Yingtai simply praised higher education as enlightenment of people's mind, which would eventually improve condition for the entire society. Master Chow was most impressed by her answer, which made her the butt of jokes by her classmates for the rest of the day.

Months went by, Master Chow gradually implemented more interesting subjects other than just the traditional classics for his small classroom of students. He also told them to practice on calligraphy, painting and to compose couplets. Yingtai and Shanbo loved to work together on the couplets, one to begin the verse and the other to wrap it up. They had so much fun doing them. For example, Shanbo would begin the couplet with: A pool of spring water reflects the sky; and Yingtai would end the couplet with: A curve of autumn moon brightens the ground.

Their growing closeness did not bother the other classmates except Ma Minchoy, who became jealous and jeeringly nicknamed them a pair of queer Mandarin ducks.

"Yingtai," Minchoy pulled Yingtai aside one day during recess in the garden and pointedly asked her. "We both come from Shaoxing. Am I right? How come I've never seen you before in a tea house…a wine shop…a gambling hall…a cock fighting pit…a swimming hole…a whore house? Why are you blushing? It's normal for us young fellows to frequent such places. But why haven't I ever met you somewhere before? Come to think of it, your face is too smooth and pretty for a man and you simply smell too nice! You must be a maiden in disguise! Come, let me find out for myself!"

Yingtai turned quickly from Minchoy but he grabbed her and tried to touch her improperly. When Shanbo saw Yingtai being assaulted by the bigger man, he ran over quickly and punched Minchoy on his face. Minchoy cried out in pain, let Yingtai go and covered his bloody nose with his sleeve. Then he turned to Shanbo with hate blazing from his eyes and snarled, "Just you wait! I'll pay you back soon!"

Shanbo told Yingtai to ignore Minchoy; saying he was just a bully wanting attention. She trembled with fright just the same, knowing her own guilty secret had almost been explosed by the rake.

As the students' level of learning had advanced, Master Chow went on to further sharpen their minds by assigning them to write dissertations on the ills affecting their society. The most interesting assignment agreed by all was on the attitude our current society had towards women.

The majority of the essays written by the class held on to the traditional view of the fair sex by Confucius, the revered philosopher in the Spring and Autumn period, whose opinion was: women and base men are equally unmanageable.

"What nonsense have most of you written about?" Master Chow was so infuriated that he used his inkwell to bang on the desk. He hit it so hard that he split the small piece of stone into two halves. "Don't you realize that by clinging to such outmoded Confucian thoughts, you are not only holding back progress in our society, but at the same time dishonoring your own mothers and sisters as well! Liang Shanbo, please stand up and read your essay to the class!"

"My title is: In Praise of Women," Shanbo stood up and read aloud. "One of the worst ills in our society is the prejudiced assessment towards women. In my humble opinion: this outmoded view is used by weak men mainly to suppress women, in order to make themselves seem more superior. Let me ask you who has given you life, carries you inside her womb for nine long months and keeps you alive and to grow strong by nursing you at her breast? Who binds your wounds when you fall and skin your knees? Who stays up late into the night to sew warm clothes to protect you from the winter cold? Who loves you no matter what faults you might have? Sure, you rely on your father to support you financially and to guide you into manhood, but you would not be able to grow properly without the orderly home your mother maintains for you! To be a good wife and mother takes hard work and intelligence. Why then do we look down on girls, deprive them the chance of being educated? Are we fools to waste the great resource in our feminine counterparts? We must uphold women as our equal in society, value them and praise them for their importance to us all!"

"Elder Brother Liang, I am so proud of you!" Yingtai whispered to Shanbo after he sat down again. "In my essay, I insist that women have the same right of men to be educated, but I have not gone so far as to praise them. I think your fabulous new theory fits right in with Chow Lo-shi's revolutionized thoughts!"

Shanbo practically glowed with Yingtai's compliment. He squeezed her hand under the desk and was rewarded with a dimpled smile from her. How come that smile made his belly tightened up into a heated knot? He kept the weird feeling to himself.

Everyone graciously congratulated Shanbo on his eye-opening article, except Ma Minchoy. The envious young man walked by and hissed, "Mama's Boy, go home!"

Chapter – 5

A Week Cruising on Xi Hu

A year went by quickly in the schoolroom of Master Chow Ming. Cool autumn days gradually replaced the hot and humid summer ones. The moon festival celebrated on the fifteenth day of the eighth lunar month was but a few days away. Master Chow decided to give the students in his small schoolroom a week of vacation. They could go home to celebrate the moon festival with their families or stay here to dine and to eat the moon cakes with him and his wife. Most of the students elected to go home, except Yingtai and Shanbo. They planned to use the break to visit Xi Hu (West Lake) and they had saved most of their allowance to finance the trip. Shanbo 's late father had taken him to a cruise on Xi Hu years ago, but he wanted to enjoy it again with Yingtai. On the other hand, Yingtai, being a young maiden, was never given the opportunity for any activities away from home. So, this trip would definitely be a wonderful adventure for both of them. The landscape of this scenic lake, famous with romantic allure, would take the entire week for them to explore.

Yingtai, Shanbo, Rensum and Sigull set out early in the morning by foot to the nearby eastern shore of Xi Hu. By dusk, they rented a small painted barge along with the service of the boatman for the week. The boat had two tiny built-in bedrooms with a dining area in-between, which accommodated them very well.

"Rensum, please share the bed with me for as long as we are on this trip!" Yingtai said to her maidservant while they unpacked the few items of clothing they had taken along for the trip.

"I'll be glad to, Young Miss!" Rensum giggled. "Just don't place a bowl of water in the middle of it!"

"I wonder if Shanbo ever has suspicion about me?" said Yingtai with a frown. "It has been tormenting for me to sleep every night next to him worrying that he might eventually discover the truth!"

Rensum gave Yingtai a crooked smile, "Young Miss, so what if he should find out you are a maiden instead of a lad? I know he loves you like a brother and I bet you he will be eager to make you his wife once he discovers the truth. You and him are truly a couple from

Heaven. He is so honorable and also good looking. You'll never find a better husband than Young Master Liang!"

"Oh, you little minx!" Yingtai playfully pinched Rensum's cheek, "You are too young to be so knowledgeable about men! Have you allowed Sigull to take advantage of you?"

Rensum turned pink at Yingtai's words. "No! But I do wish he would! Even though I have purposely allowed him opportunities to discover my true identity, he still has no clue. His head is as thick as a block of wood!"

"Shame on you!" Yingtai laughed out loud, "I must confess I feel the same way about Shanbo; he is simply too handsome a man for me not to have unchaste thoughts. With him only a bowl of water away, it takes all my fortitude not to give in to temptation!"

"Young Miss, I have a suggestion for you!" Rensum became thoughtful at Yingtai's confession. "Since you and Young Master Liang will be spending a lot of time together this week, this is the perfect opportunity to let him know the truth. You are already seventeen years old and more than ripe for marriage. It won't surprise me that your parents will shortly summon you home to be married to a total stranger they have picked out for you. Ask Young Master Liang to contact his mother; to engage a matchmaker as soon as possible to seek your hand in marriage before it is too late!"

"I'll think about what you have just suggested to me." Replied Yingtai seriously. "But I worry that if he knows, he might be furious with me for deceiving him this past year. Also, how can I be sure that he will want to wed me; a maiden who is so bold that she dares to share a bed with a man who is not her husband? I have made a very serious mistake. Unless he truly loves me, Rensum, I can't count on any commitment from him!"

"Young Miss, you worry too much!" Rensum rubbed Yingtai's shoulders to comfort her. "I think Young Master Liang has fallen in love with you without realizing you are a woman. If you observe him carefully, you can see the agonizing conflict within his eyes whenever he glances at you. The poor man must be thinking he has desire for another man!"

"Oh, Rensum! You are bad! You are too worldly-wise for one so young!" Yingtoi playfully scolded her beloved maidservant, who was barely sixteen years old.

"Young Miss, I have to be bad in order to survive!" Rensum scoffed. "Do you know what it's like to be a maidservant, even one in a good household like yours? A maidservant can be given away as a concubine to an old man already has a foot in the grave, or to a poor farmer who wants a wife just to share his miserable life of toil! If I could have my choice, I would like to marry Sigull and join Young Master Liang's household when you become his wife!"

"Don't worry! I promise you I'll take you along if Shanbo weds me. Anyway, you don't have to marry Sigull to join our household, unless you truly love him!" It was Yingtai's turn to comfort Rensum. "You are very dear to me. I'll never leave you behind!"

"Oh, thank you!" Rensum felt so relieved that she hugged Yingtai hard. "I think I do love Sigull. I sense there is a soft heart hidden within that tough hide of his!"

Shanbo had a hard time falling asleep, Sigull's thunder-like snoring below him did not help. He sorely missed feeling Yingtai's warmth close to him in the bed. Sure, the silly goose always placed that blasted bowl of water between them, but that did not prevent his hand from inching over to lightly touch a silky cheek or a soft shoulder and to breathe in whiffs of fragrance during the long nights. "I have become totally mad by falling in love with another man!" thought Shanbo. "I know Yingtai's feeling will be hurt if I request to change roommate after our vacation is over. However, I have no choice! My urge to embrace him has become so strong that it is sheer torture to lie so close to him nightly without succumbing to my desire. I would rather die a painful death by thousand cuts than to violate him, who is like a beloved younger brother to me!"

After tossing and turning half the night, Shanbo finally went to find a robe Yingtai had repaired a seam for him the day before. He clutched the garment against his face, imagining a soft hand caressing him and finally fell into an uneasy slumber.

Early next morning, they enjoyed a simple breakfast of fried dough and rice porridge provided by the boatman while being poled towards the Winery Yard and Lotus Pool in the northwest of the lake. Getting closer, they breathed in the fragrance of the lotus flowers along with the intoxicating aroma of wine drifting through the still warm autumn air. Unfolding in front of their eyes were many varieties of lotus flowers dancing in the wind, a sight so lovely that would bring out the romantic streak from everyone's heart.

"The white lotus blossom reminds me of Xi Shi, it retains its purity out of the muddy water. Xi Zhi, our beautiful heroine in the Spring/Autumn Period, who had sacrificed herself and the love of Fan Li for the sake of king and country!" Said Yingtai dreamily to Shanbo. They were leaning over the railing on one side of the painted barge, shoulder to shoulder, to take in the view of the lovely lotus blossoms.

"If I was Fan Li and you were Xi Shi, I would rather give up king and country than making a sacrifice out of my beloved woman!" Shanbo blurted out his feeling and reached for Yingtai's hand.

"Oh! Don't be silly, Elder Brother Liang!" Yingtai pulled her hand quickly out from Shanbo's warm fist. "You can't compare me to Xi Shi because I am not a woman!"

"Sorry, Younger Brother Zhu, the beauty of these lotus blossoms has mesmerized me!" Said Shanbo shamefacedly, he really wished Yingtai was a woman.

Immediately, Yingtai regretted the lost opportunity to confess her deception to Shanbo; this would have been the best romantic moment to do so. However, even with the warning from her wise maidservant fresh on her mind, she just could not bring herself to open up to Shanbo yet. She feared he might reject her outright and she could not bear the thought of losing him as a friend.

Next day, the boatman took them to the West Outer Lake, where they went on shore to visit an imperial pavilion, an octagonal pavilion, the platform over the lake and the Calligraphy and Painting Gallery. It was a bit too much sightseeing for a day.

By nightfall, they returned to the painted barge and stayed by the West Outer Lake just to view the famous 'Moon over the Peaceful Lake in Autumn'. Because it was the night of the Moon Festival, the friendly boatman served them mooncakes and plum wine with their supper. They saw with delight the autumn moon was huge and extremely bright that night, reflecting on the water of the lake like a big silver platter.

"This reflection of silvery moon on the lake reminds me of the famous Tang poet Li Bai, who had been so drunk that he drowned while trying to catch the moon in the water with his hands!" Said Yingtai with melancholy feeling. "What a tragic end for a man with such a brilliant mind! What a waste of great talent! If he had lived longer, the world would benefit from a lot more of his wonderful poetry!"

"No need to feel so downcast, he had written more than enough great poems, especially while he was drunk. That had been the reason why he was nicknamed 'Drunken Immortal' by the literary society in his time!" Shanbo tried to lighten Yingtai's mood. "Let me recite for you the 'Song of Pure Peace' written by Li Bai in praise of Yang Yuhuan, Emperor Xuanzong's beloved Precious Concubine!"

Stanza – 1

The clouds liken your clothing and the flowers your looks,
Blossoms sparkle in dew when spring breeze caresses the rails.
If I do not see you atop the Jade Mountain today,
Then I will meet you under the moonbeam someday.

Stanza – 2

You are like a peony flower fragrant with dew,
The Goddess on Wu Mountain has just lost her appeal.
Who in Han Palace can compare with your looks?
Only Flying Swallow can, after she preens her looks.

Stanza – 3

Rare flowers and ravishing women are both pleasing,
For the emperor who looks upon them is always beaming.
His boundless grief will be dissolved by the spring breeze,
While he leans on the rail north of Sandalwood Pavilion at ease.

"Thank you, Elder Brother Liang!" Yingtai laughed out loud. "I could never guess you are such a romantic! The combination of this silvery moon reflection on the lake and your recital of Li Bai's sentimental poem has definitely knocked the moodiness off me!"

29

"No need to thank me! Thank my good nature!" Shanbo drank a couple more cups of plum wine and felt really happy. He looked at Yingtai sitting across the small dining table from him and thought he saw an alluring maiden smiling at him. He rose unsteadily and reached to embrace the lovely phantom. His mouth tasted petal-soft lips and his hands found a yielding body. "Why? I think you are even more beautiful than Yang Yuhuan! Look at that jade-white oval face, those luminous eyes and the cherry-red mouth! Your looks give the word sensuality true meaning! Any mortal man won't hesitate to give up his life for a night in your arms!"

"Stop! Elder Brother Liang, you are drunk!" Yingtai fought to free herself from Shanbo's overly enthusiastic embrace. "Sigull, come quickly! Put your drunken Young Master to bed!"

Rensum came to help Sigull to take Shanbo back to his small bedroom. Then she came back out to make sure her own Young Miss was unhurt.

"Young Miss, I think you are making a mistake by not letting Young Master Liang know the truth! Look at how lovesick he has become and don't know what to do about it! You are driving him insane thinking he is in love with a man!" Rensum handed Yingtai a wet towel to wipe the sticky wine stains Shanbo had left on her face and clothing.

"Don't worry! I'll tell him everything in good time!" Yingtai felt extremely tired all of a sudden and wanted to think of nothing more than falling into bed.

However, once she was in bed, the recollection of Shanbo's hot mouth on her lips and his hands on her body kept her wide awake. She tossed and turned until Rensum became annoyed and went to sleep on the floor instead in the bed next to her.

"Since I have given Shanbo the opportunity to touch me so intimately, in theory, I am no longer a chaste maiden!" Thought Yingtai miserably. "If he refuses to wed me, I'll have no choice but to join a nunnery or end my life with a silken cord! All the advanced learning I have obtained thus far can't change the fact who I really am; a traditional young woman from an honorable family!"

Shanbo awakened to a splitting headache and felt as though he had swallowed a mouthful of ashes. Then the erotic memories surfaced to his still fuzzy brain and made him wishing for more of them. He turned to fondle the temptress who had given him such intense pleasure and was shocked to encounter Sigull instead.

"Sigull, why are you sleeping in my bed?" Shanbo yelled furiously.

"Young Master, I have been up all night wiping the sweat off your brow. I am sorry I've fallen asleep while doing that!" Sigull yawned deeply. "I think you better wash up and go to apologize to Young Master Zhu as soon as possible. You were so drunk last evening that you did some horrible things to him!"

"What?" Shanbo's head almost exploded by the alarm bell ringing inside his befuddled brain. "You mean the lovely maiden I had kissed and fondled was not real? Heaven help me, I have committed the unpardonable sin of molesting my best friend!"

"Aw, don't be so hard on yourself! You had been dead drunk last evening and Young Master Zhu is undeniably too gorgeous looking for a man! I mean not just him, but his servant as well. Rensum has such a pretty face and soft little hands! Many a time I have been tempted to sneak up on him and find out the truth for myself. I really wonder if both of them are maidens in disguise as men?"

"Well, if Yingtai is a maiden, that would be the answer to my prayers to Heaven!" Said Shanbo dreamily. "He is not just beautiful to look upon, but highly intelligent as well. What a perfect couple we will make!"

"Young Master, you might as well yearn for the moon! I wish the Old Lord is still alive. He would no doubt take you to visit Peach Blossom Pavilion, to cool down your heat with the service of their 'talented girls' there!" Sigull grunted. He worried that Old Mistress would blame him if something should go awry with her precious only son. "Please go apologize to Young Master Zhu. Then we can enjoy some breakfast before doing more sightseeing!"

After Shanbo's awkward apology during breakfast, Yingtai finally gathered enough courage to overcome her own embarrassment to suggest they should visit the famous Lingyin Si (Monastery of the Hidden Souls) today. From there they could also see the Feilai Feng (Peak that Flew from Afar).

It was a fascinating sight for them to see. The rock walls of the mountain where the monastery was built on had been carved with about 300 sculptures and inscriptions, the earliest figure was thought to date from the year 951. Past a group of three Buddhist deities at the right-hand entrance to the Qinlin cave was the monastery.

"My late father told me on our last visit that there were up to 3,000 monks living in the 18 pavilions and 75 temple halls on the mountain peak of this Lingyin Si. Can you imagine that?" Shanbo told Yingtai. He still felt a bit uneasy being alone with Yingtai; Sigull and Rensum had elected to remain on the painted-barge to do some fishing. Ever since his drunken blunder last evening, whenever he glanced his friend's way, he imagined seeing an exquisite maiden, with a peach blossom face and a luscious body under the loose robe.

"Why don't we walk around a bit, pray at the statue of the Buddha Sakyamuni and then eat our noon-rice in their vegetarian kitchen?" Yingtai suggested. She noticed how awkward Shanbo was still around her, not that she herself felt any easier after last evening's near-disaster episode. Oh, the way he stared at her, whenever he thought she was unaware had her secretly blushing; he was stripping her naked with his eyes!

Abbot Mochin (Free-of-dust) saw two large Monarch butterflies flying through the temple doorway and thought what a lovely sight they had made. Their wings were brightly patterned in tawny and black, and the way the tips of them linked together made the two butterflies appeared to be inseparable.

"Very good! Very good!" Abbot Mochin laughed out loud, which was out of character for him. "Buddha is compassionate! He gives even the smallest creatures the capacity to love and to be loved in return!"

Then he blinked and saw instead of the butterflies, there were two handsome scholars strolling towards him, their long tawny robes wafting around by the wind. Quickly, he fingered the string of beads on his chest and made a calculation. "Aha! So, they are the pair of immortal butterflies in my dream and they had been banished from Heaven for negligence of duty! Out of the kindness of my heart, I must tell them to remain true to each other, as their coming adversity will only be transient!"

"Good morrow, Holy Teacher!" Shanbo And Yingtai bowed to the ancient monk with a long white beard in front of them. "We are here to pray for guidance and blessing from the All Merciful Buddha."

32

"Good morrow to you too, Benefactors!" Replied the ancient monk. "I am Abbot Mochin. When you pray to the Buddha, be sure to ask for everlasting love for each other and that your suffering on this red-dust be short!"

After his abrupt advice to the two young scholars, Abbot Mochin simply bowed, turned and disappeared behind the massive statue of Buddha. Shanbo and Yingtai looked at each other, too stunned to stop the ancient monk to question the meaning of his unusual advice.

They approached the base of the statue of Buddha; each dropped several pieces of silver into a small basket on the long, narrow table and picked up two sticks of incense. They lit the incense sticks and inserted them into a large urn on the middle of the table, and knelt down on the cushions placed on the floor.

"All Merciful Buddha, please give me a clue as how to solve my present dilemma!" Shanbo prayed. "I have been taught that it is a crime against nature for one man to love another man. However, I don't know why my love for Zhu Yingtai feels so natural. Please help me! I would rather suffer a death of thousand cuts than to give him up!"

"Compassionate Buddha, I am a headstrong maiden who needs your guidance!" Yingtai prayed. "To prove my conviction that women are equal to men, my impetuous behavior has landed me in a situation of which my womanly virtue will become questionable. Please show me a way to let Liang Shanbo, the man I love, to know of my true identity without risking rejection from him!"

They held hands when they rose from their knees and faced each other. There was no need of words to express what had been hidden within their hearts. Shanbo wiped Yingtai's tears off her cheeks tenderly with his sleeve and she laid her forehead briefly on his shoulder. Still hand in hand, they headed for the vegetarian kitchen to eat their noon-rice.

Chapter – 6

A Sentimental Farewell

After doing some more sightseeing such as listening to Orioles Singing in the Willows, Viewing the Fish at Flower Pond and visiting the Peony Garden centering on the Peony Pavilion, Shanbo and Yingtai along with their attendants made their way home one early morning to Master Chow's boarding house. However, as soon as the tired travelers had arrived, they were met by a very anxious Madam Chow.

"Young Master Zhu," Madam Chow handed a letter from her father to Yingtai. "I am afraid there is bad news for you. The manservant who brought this message from your home told me your mother has fallen ill!"

Her father's message was very brief. It said only, "To my daughter Yingtai: Your mother is sick. Come home immediately!"

"Go say farewell to your teacher and classmates before you leave." Madam Chow told Yingtai. "I'll ask Cook to pack a picnic lunch for you to eat on your road home."

"Thank you so much!" Yingtai thank her warmly. "You have been like a mother to me this past year and I'll never forget you!"

With a heavy heart, Yingtai went to bid farewell to her teacher and classmates, and sent Rensum up to their bedroom to pack their few belongings. She knew in her heart that once she was home, no matter what condition her mother's health was in, her father would never allow her to return here again. That was the reason why she had avoided going home during last Lunar New Year holiday.

Master Chow was genuinely sad to see one of his best pupils go. "Yingtai, I hope your mother gets better and you can return to us soon! I am going to miss your compelling discussions on my lectures!"

All her classmates except Ma Minchoy came up to wish her mother well and hope for her early return to school. The bully just sat at his desk grinning at her.

As Yingtai turned to leave the classroom, Minchoy suddenly shot up from his desk and barred her way.

"Yingtai!" Minchoy gave her a wide smile, grabbed both her hands and placed them against his chest. "Don't worry about your mother, I think she is very well! I've found out who you really are and won't let you escape from me this time. Let me assure you we'll meet again during the Lunar New Year holidays!"

Yingtai pulled her hands from Minchoy's grasp and quickly left the classroom, her face reddened with embarrassment. The bully's shrill laughter followed her all the way out the door.

Despite protest from Yingtai, Shanbo insisted that he and Sigull would walk with her and Rensum all the way to the farewell gazebo, several miles away, where they would eat their noon-rice before saying goodbye. Secretly, Yingtai was glad that Shanbo showed his care for her. She had fallen head over heels in love with her handsome classmate and roommate, and felt miserable that he would be lost to her shortly. Oh! How could she bear not to see him or lie close to him nightly ever again? How could she bear to be married to a complete stranger after a year of companionship with this gentle-natured scholar?

Yingtai told Rensum that she would help her carry some of their belongings. Rensum declined and said, "Sigull wants to carry the two reed baskets for us until we reach the farewell gazebo. Young Miss, guess what else? He told me how much he would miss me and that if I had a sister who looked even a little bit like me, he would definitely want her to be his wife!"

Sigull's remark to Rensum made Yingtai thoughtful; merciful Buddha had answered her prayer after all.

Shanbo and Yingtai intentionally walked a lengthy distance behind Sigull and Rensum, they wanted to have some private time with each other. Shanbo gave Yingtai his hand when they had to cross a narrow plank over a stream and they continued holding hands after the crossing.

"Look! Elder Brother Liang, there is a pair of Mandarin ducks playing in the pond!" Yingtai gushed, the road was full of scenic spots. "Do you think they are both males?"

"Don't be silly, Younger Brother Zhu!" Shanbo laughed and squeezed Yingtai's hand. "Mandarin ducks are love birds, always one male and one female to make a pair. Look how they cross their necks together while swimming! I wish we were them, don't you?"

Yingtai squeezed Shanbo's hand in return and leaned closer to him, inhaling deeply his manly scent of sweat and pine soap. "Yes, my wonderful Elder Brother Liang! Unfortunately, we are both males and can't make a loving pair of Mandarin ducks!"

"That's so unfair!" moaned Shanbo. "You should have been born a woman, so that we can be a loving couple too!"

"Don't feel bad!" Yingtai comforted Shanbo, laying a hand on his shoulder. "I have a twin sister at home who looks just like me. Would you like me to act as the matchmaker for you?"

"Yes, of course! If she has half of your looks, she will definitely be beautiful!" Shanbo's face lit up like the sun. He felt so joyful that he forgot decorum and wrapped Yingtai in a tight embrace. All a sudden he realized that he was not pressing another man's hard chest against his own, but the yielding bosom of a woman. And this time he had not imbibed any plum wine! Sheer joy blossomed from his heart with that realization. So, he had not been in love with another man after all, but with an exquisite maiden!

"Aha! The little minx was so shy that she attempted to cover up with the excuse of having a twin sister!" Shanbo thought. "No wonder she placed that blasted bowl of water nightly in the middle of the bed to keep me away from her! Also, she blamed those tiny holes in her earlobes as the ploy by her mother to fool the evil spirits into believing her son was a daughter! Why was I such an idiot? Sleeping in the same bed with her for the past year, I could have seduced her and claimed her as mine. But instead of having her naked and willing in my arms, I tortured myself with the belief that I was in love with a man!"

Yingtai felt her bones crumbled within Shanbo's tight embrace and the joyful look on his handsome face melted her heart. She could not hold back her yearning for him any longer. Forgetting shame, she pulled him abruptly under the dense, leafy shelter of a clump of weeping willows and kissed him. He responded by pressing her down to the ground with him.

"My beloved Yingtai, are you that twin sister you wish me to wed?" Shanbo whispered into Yingtai's ear as he caressed her, his touch set her body aflame.

"Shanbo, I am sorry I have deceived you! I was afraid you would reject me for being indecent, for dared to share a bed with a man who was not my husband!"

"Ah! So, you were that shameless hussy who seduced me nightly, then cooled down my lust with a bowl of cold water!"

"Be serious! I did consider enter a nunnery or hang myself with a silken cord if you don't want me!"

"My precious Yingtai, how can you think such a thing? I loved you even when I thought you were a man! Please believe I will love you until the seas run dry and the mountains crumble to dust!"

They pulled apart reluctantly and stood up when they heard Rensum's excited voice, telling them the farewell gazebo was in sight. Straightening each other's clothing, their hands shook with unfulfilled desire.

Shanbo kissed Yingtai's swollen lips once more and whispered into her ear, "We have only licked a little honey from the cake. Wait until I get you into the marriage bed; I'll show you how to stir clouds and rains with me!"

The picnic lunch Madam Chow packed for them was simple but filling. They ate sticky rice streamed with black mushrooms and pork sausage, and enjoyed homemade almond cookies as well. Then it was time for Yingtai and Rensum to continue their journey home.

Holding hands, Yingtai whispered to Shanbo, "Beloved, please send a message to your mother and ask her to arrange for a matchmaker before Lunar New Year. If you don't, I have a premonition that it would be too late for us!"

"Don't worry, My Precious Love, I'll write to my mother tonight!" Shanbo squeezed Yingtai's hand to reassure her, he felt his heart was breaking to see her go. "I hope your mother recovers soon to see her daughter marrying a man who loves her madly!"

Rensum and Sigull came out of the farewell gazebo together, they too had been reluctant to part from each other. Unable to delay their journey home any longer, Yingtai and Rensum bowed to Shanbo and Sigull, and turned away from them with tears in their eyes.

Chapter – 7

The Betrothal

By the time Yingtai and Rensum reached home, the cooking smokes were visible on the horizon. They did not enter the house from the front, but climbed the stone steps at the right side up to the small terrace garden on the second level, leading straight into Yingtai's private quarters. There they hastily changed from their male disguise into feminine clothing before going downstairs to see Yingtai's parents.

Just as Yingtai suspected, her mother was not ill but appeared hale and hearty. It was just a ruse to get her to return home quickly. And she was sitting with her father at the dinner table, preparing to eat their evening-rice. They smiled broadly when they saw their daughter and her maidservant coming into the dining room.

"Papa and Mama," Yingtai kneeled down to venerate her parents. "Your unfilial daughter is home!"

"I hope you are done with your wanderlust!" Said Squire Zhu sternly to their daughter. "From now on I expect you to stay home to practice skills more befitting a maiden!"

"Get up! Get up! Come sit down to eat! You must be hungry!" Madam Zhu rolled her eyes at her husband and pulled Yingtai to her feet.

Then she turned to their daughter's maidservant and said, "Rensum, you too go to eat your evening-rice in the kitchen! You must be very tired after tilting those two reed baskets all the way home!"

"Old Mistress, thank you for your concern! Young Miss did help me with the luggage part of the way!" Rensum also kneeled down to kowtow to her master and mistress before she left for the kitchen.

Yingtai sat down at the round dining table across from her parents while a servant put down a pair of chopsticks and a porcelain spoon in front of her, and served her a bowl of rice and a small tureen of winter melon soup. She drank the soup and waited for her parents to finish picking out their selections from the dishes of food laying out on the table into their rice bowls before getting them for herself.

38

She was happy to see Cook had concocted some of her favorite dishes and ate with gusto. There were chunks of tofu stir-fried with fresh spinach in an oyster sauce; fried eggs with chopped string-beans; crispy chicken stir-fried with peanuts and bits of black mushrooms in a sweet plum sauce; and small bowls of almond flavored custard for dessert.

After the evening meal, they went out to the front courtyard to catch the cool breeze before retiring to bed. Madam Zhu's maidservant Dongmui served everyone a cup of Dragon Well tea to aid digestion. After he finished drinking his cup of tea, Squire Zhu went to walk around the flowerbeds to inspect the chrysanthemums.

Yingtai became drowsy sitting next to her mother and could not hold back a yawn.

"Daughter," Madam Zhu put her arm around Yingtai's shoulders and said. "Go ahead to bed, you must be so tired. Umm...We have important news for you tomorrow!"

Yingtai became instantly wide-awake, alerted by her mother's heavy tune of voice.

"Mama, what's the important news?" asked Yingtai anxiously. "Tell me now or I won't be able to sleep a wink tonight!"

"Your father is seriously considering a marriage proposal from one of his important business associates for his only son!"

"Oh no, Mama, I don't want to get married!"

"You are already seventeen. You want to be an old maid?"

"Mama, please! I'll marry, but to someone I love!"

"Are you out of your mind? Your father will disown you if he finds out you are not chaste!"

"Don't worry, Mama, I am still very much a virgin! However, I've already promised myself to one of my classmates and I'll not break my vow to him!"

"Guanyin, Goddess of Mercy, please save us! You mean a man has uncovered your disguise? Tell me it's not true! This is a disaster! By law, if a young woman is convicted of involvement with a man outside marriage, she could be sentenced to drown in the river!"

"How about those prostitutes servicing men in the pleasure houses, have any of them been put to death by drowning previously?"

"No! Prostitutes are outcasts in our society; therefore, they are not punishable by law for fornication. Shame on you! Where on Earth have you picked up such improper knowledge?"

39

"I learned from discussions on social problems in the classroom. Prostitution is one of the worst social problems affecting women!"

"Forget about the whores! Let me ask you who is the man you are involved with?"

"Mama, his given name is Shanbo, an only son from the house of Liang. His late father was our previous magistrate of Shaoxing."

"Umm...he comes from a highly esteemed but now impoverished family. Magistrate Liang was well known for being an honest official with two sleeves full of clean breeze!"

"So, you don't have any objection for Shanbo to be your son-in-law?"

"No, I don't if he is diligent and has aspiration to follow his late father's footsteps! No one should measure a young man's potential by the ups and downs of his family's fortune!"

"Oh! Thank you, Mama!"

"Don't thank me yet! The other young man who seeks your hand in marriage is also an only son but from a fabulously rich and influential family. Your father has a lot of business dealings with his father and therefore, he can't afford to antagonize the Ma family!"

"What are you saying? You say his last name is Ma?"

"That's right, Daughter! His name is Ma Minchoy. The matchmaker from the Ma family hinted that Ma Minchoy had somehow met you by chance and had become totally mesmerized by your beauty!"

"Ai-ya, Mama! Ma Minchoy is one of my classmates and he is a spoiled brat and a bully to boot! I think he has somehow found out my true identity and once even tried to molest me. I would rather be an old maid or even a nun than being his wife! Please refuse outright the marriage proposal from the Ma family!"

"Silly Girl, I wish it could be so simple! Best let your father discuss the situation with you tomorrow. Don't upset him with anything tonight!"

Poor Yingtai became so worried from what her mother had so casually informed her, that despite she was bone-tired, she tossed and turned in bed all through the night.

"Papa, I would rather die than be Ma Minchoy's wife!" Yingtai pleaded with her father next morning after breakfast, she knew her father was always feeling more mellow with a full belly.

"Shameless Chit!" Squire Zhu scolded. "How dare you promise yourself to a man without your parents' permission and a matchmaker's proposal of a bride price? The Ma family has offered one thousand ounces of gold for your hand in marriage. Could the Liang family top that?"

"I don't mean to show disrespect, but you know very well Liang Shanbo's family has fallen into hard times after his father's death. Poor Lady Liang will never be able to scrape one tenth of that amount, even if she sells what little holdings left by her late husband!"

"Ai-ya, my Heart-and-Liver!" Squire Zhu softened and gave his beloved daughter a wry smile. "You think I care about the mountain of gold the Ma family wants to buy you for their spoiled son? No, Daughter, I much rather wed you to Liang Shanbo, a scion from an impovished but honorable family. Unfortunately, I can't afford to antagonize them at the moment, due to they are holding a lien against our wineries. We had a failed harvest last autumn!"

"I am sorry to hear that, Papa!" Yingtai appreciated her father's candor. "But if you inform them subtly that your daughter has already promised to another, won't they be satisfied and withdraw their offer for my hand?"

"Daughter, for your sake I am going to try!" Squire Zhu looked at his daughter with so much love in his eyes that made Yingtai wanted to weep. "However, don't hold your hopes too high! We are dealing with one of the richest and most powerful families in this area. They are even related to our current magistrate. Whatever they want, they usually get!"

Yingtai had to be contented with what her father promised her. She spent her days waiting for the coming of Liang Shanbo's matchmaker by sewing and embroidering a trousseau, working mostly on cold weather wearables. She hoped to become his wife by the Lunar New Year, which would only be three short months away.

Shanbo asked Sigull to pack up their belongings in preparation for their journey home. He had already said his farewell to his teacher and fellow classmates and was looking forward to reunite with Yingtai in matrimony during Lunar New Year, just a few weeks away. His heart was bubbling with joy, anticipating a lifetime living with the woman he loved.

41

"Young Master Liang," Madam Chow called to Shanbo. "Come, eat a bowl of hot rice congee to warm you up before you leave! It's getting really chilly now so near Lunar New Year!"

"Thank you, Madam Chow!" Shanbo sat down to a spread of hot rice congee and side dishes of chopped pork sausages, pickled radishes and fried dough sticks. He ate with gusto while Madam Chow beamed at him.

Madam Chow asked Shanbo with concern, "Master Chow told me you are not returning to class next year. Is everything alright at home?"

"Please don't worry, everything is fine!" Shanbo laughed gaily. "I am just going home to get married. I don't plan to come back to school because I want to compete in the official scholastic examination come spring. I need to obtain a minor official position to support my family!"

"You are a good boy! Who is the lucky bride?"

"Ha! Ha! Ha! You mean you have not guessed? My future wife is Zhu Yingtai, my classmate and roommate for the past year!"

"No! I always thought Young Master Zhu was too beautiful and fragile looking for a man, but never actually guessed he was a maiden in disguise!"

"Well, I just found that out for myself two months ago when we bade each other farewell on her way home!"

"How about that! I must tell Master Chow this news right away! He'll be delighted to know two of his most brilliant pupils are getting married!"

"I shouldn't have told you! Please just keep this to yourselves! The fact that my future wife has been in the company of young men might cause a scandal!"

"Ai-ya, don't worry! Except for my husband, I won't tell a soul! By the way, Ma Minchoy is returning home to get married too. What a coincidence!"

Hearing that Ma Minchoy was also returning home to wed, Shanbo felt uneasy all of a sudden. Then he shrugged his shoulders and said to Madam Chow, "Best of luck for the young maiden who is getting him for a husband!"

Yingtai put down the red silk bridal jacket she was embroidering. The complicated pattern of intertwining pink peony flowers, green leaves,

42

silver clouds and golden bats was making her eyes itch. She had to finish it quickly though, just in case her future mother-in-law, Lady Liang, wanted to set an early date for her son's wedding.

But where was the matchmaker Shanbo promised her that his mother would send? Please Guanyin, Goddess of Mercy, let her not be late! Her father had told her that if Shanbo's matchmaker did not show up within next week, he would have no choice but to accept the Ma family's offer of betrothal for her hand.

She would rather be dead than being that bully's wife!

Shanbo's enthusiastic homecoming went flat.

"Mama, please say that again!" Shanbo tearfully begged his mother. "Tell me it's not true that you haven't sent a matchmaker to the Zhu family yet!"

"Calm down!" Lady Liang ordered her beloved son, her heart was breaking seeing how upset he had become. "I had already approached several matchmakers on your behalf, to make an offer for the hand of Young Miss Zhu. However, none of them wanted to represent us. They said it would be a waste of their time and effort. Their reason was this, that we could never hope to compete with the rich and powerful Ma family, who had already made an offer for Young Miss Zhu, with a bride price of one thousand ounces in gold!"

"You don't know Yingtai, Mama, she is not the type of girl who cares about money! I love her with all my heart! I know she'll never agree to marry Ma Minchoy, the bully she loathes!"

"Son, listen to me!" Lady Liang tenderly cupped her son's face with her hands. "You are still young for a man. Don't worry about getting married until you have established yourself. Then there will be many beautiful maidens you can choose a wife from! Why torture yourself over just one Young Miss Zhu? Besides, I don't think a maiden who has been bold enough to impersonate a man will make a proper wife! I know you'll get over her soon!"

"Oh, Mama! You don't understand!" Shanbo became hysterical. "I'll die if Yingtai is lost to me!"

Lady Liang gave up reasoning with her son. She thought he was experiencing a pang of puppy-love. She told Sigull to put his Young Master early to bed and hoped that he would calm down after a good night's sleep.

43

Chapter – 8

Meeting on the Terrace Garden

"Young Master, where are we going so early in the morning?" Sigull rubbed sleep from his eyes and yawned. He did not sleep well last night due to he was listening to Shanbo's sobbing half the night.

"I am going to the Zhu family home to visit Yingtai!" Shanbo told Sigull with a tilted-up chin, he looked terrible with his eyes puffy and bloodshot. "I want to hear from her own mouth that she wants to marry Ma Minchoy instead of me!"

"I don't think they'll let you visit with an unmarried maiden!"

"I'll ask to see their Young Master Zhu, my classmate!"

"Umm…that might work! I wonder how pretty Rensum will look in woman's clothing?"

"I am sure she will look ravishing, just like her Young Miss!"

"You think Rensum will want to marry me?

"You'll have to ask her yourself!"

"I sure hope Young Miss Zhu becomes your wife, so that Rensum can come along with her!"

"I think we better get going before my mother wakes up. I don't think she will approve what I am about to do!"

Rensum opened the front door to unusual loud pounding. She was surprised to see Sigull standing outside and Young Master Liang was walking back and forth across the lane, under the three weeping willow trees.

"Elder Brother Sigull and Young Master Liang, please come in!" Rensum blushed, Sigull was staring at her with his mouth popped wide open.

"Rensum, you are looking very pretty!" Shanbo gave his servant a stern look and complimented the young maidservant courteously. "Please let your Young Miss know I am here to see her!"

"Young Master Liang, you are in luck!" Rensum smiled and curtsied to Shanbo. "Both Old Master and Old Mistress are not home. Please come around to the right side of the house and climb up the steps to the terrace garden. It will lead you directly to Young Miss's private quarters!"

Yingtai sat alone brooding in the terrace garden, under the arbor of white jasmine vines. It had been three days since the Ma family had sent over the marriage contract for her father's signature and this morning they had also sent over a cartload of small red wedding cakes filled with a sweet paste of lotus seeds. And right now, her parents were somewhere in town purchasing new furniture to complete her dowry. Where was that matchmaker Shanbo had promised her? She heaved a deep sigh and thought dejectedly of a bleak future as Ma Minchoy's wife.

Shanbo climbed up the stairs to the terrace garden alone, Sigull wanted to stay with Rensum in the kitchen, helping her to fix a tea tray. He was anxious to see his beloved Yingtai and to explain to her his mother's problem with the matchmakers.

The sight of the beautiful maiden sitting under the jasmine arbor took Shanbo's breathe away. She was dressed in a quilted gown of pink and silver brocade, with a white silk peony flower struck on the side of her raven hair cloud. Could this fairy-looking creature be his beloved classmate and roommate of the past year? He walked towards her with a wide smile and was unpleasantly surprised by the fury he saw flashing from her eyes.

"My Precious Love, I am so glad to see you!" Shanbo tried to embrace Yingtai.

"Don't you dare touch Ma Minchoy's betrothed! You have come three days too late!" Yingtai wanted to cut out her deceitful lover's lying tongue.

"Please, Yingtai, let me explain!" Shanbo grabbed Yingtai and kissed her passionately. "My mother was unable to find even one matchmaker who wanted to represent us, to compete with the rich and powerful Ma family for your hand! This is the reason I come to see you directly. If possible, I would like to speak to your father directly and ask for his permission to wed you!"

"Haven't I already told you, that you are three days too late?" Yingtai started to cry, her tears soaked through the cotton material on Shanbo's chest.

"Aw...you can't mean that! You have already told me you will marry me and I am holding you to your promise!" Shanbo began to feel panicky, the ground was shifting under his feet.

"I am sorry to tell you it's true!" Yingtai said despairingly. "My father has no choice but to give me to Ma Minchoy because he is under serious financial obligation to the Ma family! The marriage contract was signed three days ago!"

"No! No! No! No! No!" Shanbo moaned like an animal in pain. Yingtai felt her heart was breaking for him. She pulled him down to sit on the stone bench and put her arms around him. He kissed her again, this time close to fury and proceeded to caress her. She knew he needed to touch her for comfort and did not have the heart to stop him. She also knew this would be the last chance for them to be together. Despairing of her own hopeless future, she made a sudden decision.

"Beloved," Yingtai said simply to Shanbo. "Come with me to my bedchamber!"

Shanbo followed Yingtai without question, he was desperate for her. She took him inside her bedchamber and locked the door.

Rensum and Sigull came up the terrace garden with a tray of tea and a plate of wedding cakes. They looked everywhere for Yingtai and Shanbo but they were nowhere in sight. Then Rensum noticed the locked bedchamber door and knew her Young Miss had made her choice.

"Come, Elder Brother Sigull!" Rensum put her hand on Sigull's arm and she blushed, thinking of the choice she had also just made. "Would you like to enjoy a cup of tea and snacks in my bedroom?"

Seeing the seductive look in Rensum's eyes, Sigull was so overjoyed that he almost dropped the tray of tea he was holding.

Shanbo and Yingtai gazed lovingly at each other. The hour they had spent inside the jasmine scented bed-box did not dissipate their passion but rather intensified it.

"My Precious Love," Shanbo kissed Yingtai tenderly. "I will never forget what you have just given me! I hope you'll not suffer at the hands of your future husband when he finds out!"

"He won't have a chance to find out! I swear to you that even though I must step into the flower palanquin his family is sending, I'll never submit to Ma Minchoy. He'll have to buy concubines to warm his bed!"

"Then I'll die happy knowing you belong only to me!"

Before parting, Yingtai gave her lover a thick strand of her long hair tied with a pink silk kerchief. Shanbo pocketed her gift but could not bear to leave her. He clung to her and wept until he choked out blood along with his tears.

Sigull was also reluctant to part from Rensum. He slapped her bottom playfully and said, "Don't worry! I am going to buy your freedom with my savings. I guarantee you'll be the most satisfied wife in Shaoxing!"

Chapter – 9

The Star-Crossed Lovers

After his parting from Yingtai on her terrace garden, Shanbo fell into a deep depression. He refused to eat or drink and wanted only to remain in bed all day with her lock of hair pressed against his face. He even called out her name in his dreams. His mother became so worried that she beat Sigull with her cane to get the truth out of him. His head was full of painful bumps before Sigull broke down and told her everything.

"What happened to Shanbo the day you and him went out without my knowledge?"

"Aw…Old Mistress, we went to visit his classmate Young Miss Zhu!"

"Was he allowed to see her?"

"We were able to get in because her parents were out shopping."

"Did you stay with Shanbo the whole time while he was there?"

"No…Old Mistress, Young Miss Zhu took him into her bedchamber for about an hour."

"You mean you allowed that shameless hussy to dally alone with my son?"

"Sorry! I wasn't able to get in, she had her bedchamber door locked!"

"No wonder Shanbo is ill! He has become lovesick yearning for another lick of what that wanton had shamelessly given him!"

"Young Master won't be able to see her anymore; she is going to be married shortly!"

"So, she is going to give her new husband my son's leavings?"

"Old Mistress, please don't say such awful things about her! I believe she really loves Young Master and she has no choice in marrying someone else!"

"Wah…Wah…Wah! She loves Shanbo so much that she is killing him from wanting her!"

Lady Liang cried until she had no tears left. Shanbo remained imperceptible to his mother's pain. He starved himself to death while calling weakly for Yingtai to come to him.

The day after Liang Shanbo had been buried, Sigull went to seek Squire Zhu's permission to buy Rensum's freedom. He feared that if the pretty maidservant went over with Young Miss Zhu to the Ma family, she would be lost to him forever. He also wanted to give Young Miss Zhu the news of Shanbo's death; he reasoned they were good friends as well as lovers.

He saw a huge crowd of gaudily dressed musicians milling around a flower palanquin in front of the Zhu's residence and realized he had come just in time. For Young Miss Zhu was about to be carried away as a new bride for Ma Minchoy, and his beloved Rensum would most likely end up as his concubine. Umm… he would not allow this to happen…unless over his dead body! He puffed his chest out and went to knock at the front door.

Sigull had no problem with Squire Zhu. In fact, the kindly elder agreed to release Rensum from bondage without taking any money from him. "Treat that as Rensum's dowry from me and my wife. We love her like a daughter!"

Sigull was overjoyed with this unexpected good fortune. While he waited for Rensum to pack her belongings, he also asked Squire Zhu if he may see Young Miss Zhu.

"I don't think this is a good time. My daughter is getting married today and the flower palanquin is already waiting outside to carry her to her new husband's family!"

"Old Master, I understand. However, I have very important news concerning my Young Master for her. They have been best friends as well as classmates!"

"All right then, but for just a moment! Look! Here she comes in her bridal finery!"

Sigull was struck dumb seeing how beautiful Zhu Yingtai looked in a red and gold outfit, her hair cloud sparkled with jeweled hairpins. How he wished his Young Master was still alive and this fairy-like maiden was going to him as a bride!

"Hello, Sigull!" Yingtai was glad to see her beloved's servant, especially because he had come for Rensum. "How is your Young Master Liang doing? I miss him a lot!"

"Wah! Wah! Wah!" Sigull lost control and bawled his heart out. "My Young Master had starved himself to death with lovesickness, two weeks after he had left you! He had also cried for you to come to him with his last breath! We just buried him yesterday!"

"Oh! No! No! No!" Yingtai felt as though a dagger was punching into her heart and the world turned dark with her pain.

When she came to, she was lying on the floor and her mother was spooning hot ginger soup into her mouth. She saw both Sigull and Rensum stood there gawking at her and the pain surged back with the horrible recollection, the sad news of her beloved Liang Shanbo.

"Mama, I want to visit Shanbo's grave!" Yingtai wailed. "I need to ask for his forgiveness! I have killed him with my love!"

"Hush! You can't do such a thing!" Madam Zhu said. "Today you are a bride wearing red bridal clothing, not at all appropriate to visit a gravesite!"

"Then please buy me a sackcloth coat with a hood, a pair of white candles and a stack of paper ghost money!" Yingtai beseeched her mother.

"Well, alright!" Madam Zhu knew she had to give in to her daughter's demand; Yingtai had always been that headstrong. "But you must wear the sackcloth coat over your bridal garment. You don't have enough time coming back here to change!"

Sorrowfully, Yingtai's parents watched their beloved daughter left home dressed like a widow to her wedding. Out of concern, Sigull and Rensum followed her.

The musicians accompanying the flower palanquin was playing funeral music instead of wedding tunes, all the way to Liang Shanbo's gravesite.

Yingtai alighted the flower palanquin at Shanbo's gravesite, the soil around the burial mound was still damp. Sigull and Rensum came over to help her to walk on the rough ground. When she reached Shanbo's tombstone, she asked them to step aside to allow her the privacy to mourn her lover.

After the pair of white candles were lit, Yingtai set ablaze the stack of paper ghost money in the fire basin. A sudden gust scattered and blew the curls of the burnt offering up into the sky, resembling a shower of silvery petals.

"Oh, my beloved Shanbo!" Yingtai kneeled down and touched the carvings of Liang Shanbo's name on the tombstone. "Please forgive me for being the instrument that had shortened your life! It would be better if we had never met! Even though I have to go to the Ma family now against my will, you will always be my only love and my true husband! How I wish you could take me to wherever you are now!"

As if the sky took pity on the sorrow of the lovesick maiden, it turned dark and ominous with a sudden gale. Then within a heartbeat, thunder and lightning came roaring in to repel the gloom. Everyone sought cover except Yingtai, she only wrapped her arms around the tombstone for support against the rising wind.

A thunderclap descended from heaven and hit the burial mound. The mound burst open and Yingtai saw Shanbo stepping out in his white burial clothing. With unrestrained joy she fought the fierce wind to go to him. They embraced amid the terrible storm.

The stunned onlookers could not believe what they had just seen with their own eyes. They held their breath when they next witnessed Shanbo held Yingtai's hand and led her into the open grave.

"Young Miss, don't go in there with him! He is already dead!" Rensum yelled to Yingtai, but her desperate cry was drowned out by the furious sounds of the storm.

"Rensum, don't worry!" Sigull held on to her. "I'll go get her out of that mound!"

However, the burial mound closed up entirely before Sigull could reach it. Then the sky suddenly brightened and the storm subsided so quickly as if it had never happened.

Everybody came out of the shelter to help then. They scooped out the soft soil of the burial mound with their bare hands and their shoes. They did not stop until they spotted the closed coffin and quickly lifted up the lid. The coffin was empty. There was no sight of either Shanbo or Yingtai's body anywhere.

Then out of the corners of their eyes, they saw a large pair of Monarch butterflies flying out of the coffin together, their beautiful tawny and black patterned wings bright with sunlight. They danced awhile on top of the astonished onlookers, then flew straight up to heaven, wingtip to wingtip.

Rensum turned to Sigull and said with tears running down her face, "We were privileged to have known them. I believe they had been reincarnated from a pair of loving butterflies!"

The pair of Monarch butterflies awakened suddenly. They found themselves resting on a large peach leaf and saw with dismay the peaches on the boughs were not golden and ripe, but small and hard like green grapes. A flash of guilty remembrance passed between them and made them squirming with shame. Then joy surged through them when they realized their missing wings had been restored.

Since there were no ripening peaches to patrol, they flew together to a nearby lotus pond to guard the lotus seeds from being eaten by the birds. Butterfly Boy suddenly made a revelation to Butterfly Girl when they were perching on the edge of a large pod.

"I dreamed that I was watching lotus blossoms as a human somewhere on Earth and you were there beside me."

"Umm...How did I look? Was I pretty like a lotus blossom?"

"To my eyes, you were more beautiful than the flower!"

"Shush! Do you want to be punished for being romantic?"

"I don't care! I just want you to love me!"

"I do love you! But the Jade Emperor has declared human emotions are symbols of weakness, unworthy of his immortals!"

"Don't let him in on our secret then! I know I will love you until the seas run dry and the mountains crumble to dust!"

"Ai-ya! Here you go again! Haven't you once declared this to me as a human? Oh, no! I had been dreaming about you too!"

After rubbing each other's antenna for a while, the pair of Monarch butterflies linked their wings together, tip to tip, and danced joyfully around the lotus blossoms. They glazed at each other frequently with bulging eyes full of longing, giddy with their guilty secret...they were in love for eternity!

The End

Dear Reader:

I hope you have enjoyed reading this Chinese version of the star-crossed lovers' Romeo and Juliet story. The romantic tale of Liang Shanbo and Zhu Yingtai is one of the most famous legends in China, beloved by both young and old. I suspect the original author had been a woman in Ancient China with a streak of rebellion in her, who was daring enough to make up a story about a female scholar.

This is the 6th Chinese historical novel I have written. If you are interested, please visit my Author page to see all my works online: https://www.amazon.com/author/teresangebooks.

Thank you!

Teresa Ng

Made in United States
North Haven, CT
17 September 2024

57507764R00029